THE SWORD OF THE SILVER KNIGHT

created by
GERTRUDE CHANDLER WARNER

Illustrated by Robert Papp

ALBERT WHITMAN & Company
Morton Grove, IL

The Sword of the Silver Knight
created by Gertrude Chandler Warner;
illustrated by Robert Papp.

ISBN 0-8075-0877-2 (hardcover)
ISBN 0-8075-0876-4 (paperback)

Cover art by Robert Papp.

For more information about Albert Whitman & Company,
visit our web site at www.albertwhitman.com.

Contents

THE SWORD OF THE
SILVER KNIGHT

CHAPTER 1

Stepping Back in Time

"You'll never believe it! There's a knight on horseback riding across the field!" called six-year-old Benny Alden, racing back to his sisters and brother.

"Benny, you have a great imagination!" said twelve-year-old Jessie.

The Alden children were on their way to Pleasant Valley Park for a picnic. The park was hidden from view by tall pine trees. But Benny had run ahead of the others. Now he had come back to tell them the exciting news.

"I'm serious!" Benny said. "There's a huge tent, and some smaller tents, and knights on horseback!"

Henry, who was fourteen, raised his eyebrows. "Oh, no! We forgot to bring our armor," he said with a smile.

The others laughed. Even Benny had to smile. But as they walked just beyond the pine trees, he pointed down to the field below. "See?" he said.

The Aldens stopped in surprise. Benny was right! A huge colorful tent, like a circus tent, filled the open field in front of them. Behind it were several smaller tents.

A man on horseback was riding from one of the smaller tents into the larger one. Just as Benny had said, the man was dressed in shining armor.

"I feel like we've stepped back in time," said Jessie.

"Look!" Violet said, pointing to a large sign that said, "Medieval Fair."

"What does m-m-med . . . what does that mean?" Benny asked. He was just learning to read.

"That was a time, hundreds of years ago, when the world was ruled by kings and queens and there were knights," Henry explained. "It's also called the Middle Ages."

According to the dates on the sign, the fair was opening that evening. "The fair will be here all week!" cried Violet.

"Awesome!" Benny said.

"And look," Jessie added, pointing to a piece of paper attached to the sign. "They need volunteers."

"I want to be a volunteer," said Benny eagerly. He paused for a moment before asking, "What is a volunteer?"

"A volunteer is someone who helps with something," Henry explained.

"We're good at helping," Jessie said.

"Let's check it out," Benny cried, running down the hill toward the main tent.

The others followed, catching up with Benny at the open doorway to the large tent. The Aldens walked cautiously inside.

"Wow!" said Benny. All four children stood and stared.

Inside the tent, long rows of tables were

arranged around a center ring. Colorful banners hung down from the ceiling of the tent.

The children paused for a moment, amazed at what they saw. Men on horseback trotted around the ring. Each man wore armor with a different colored jersey—red, green, blue, gold, or purple—and a matching cape that flowed gracefully behind him. But the Aldens were most impressed by a tall man who wore a silver jersey to match his shining armor.

"I like the silver knight best," said Benny, pointing.

A tall thin woman approached them. She had glasses and short brown hair that curved around her face. Unlike the others in the ring, she was dressed in modern clothes, a light blue skirt with a white blouse.

"Hello," she said, smiling at the children. "I'm Hannah Greene. I'm the manager here."

"We're the Aldens," Henry said. "I'm Henry. These are my sisters, Jessie and

Violet, and my brother, Benny."

"We live close to here, Ms. Greene," Jessie explained. "We were planning to have a picnic in the park, but . . ."

"But you found out it had been taken over by a medieval fair?" Ms. Greene asked, smiling kindly. "Please, call me Hannah."

"This is totally cool!" Benny said with excitement.

"I'm glad you think so," said Hannah. "We open tonight, and we're hoping lots of people will think it's cool."

"What exactly goes on at a medieval fair?" Henry asked.

"We put on a wonderful show," Hannah explained. "The knights are warming up for it right now. They joust and do battle, and in the end one knight wins the hand of a beautiful princess."

Violet's eyes were shining. "That does sound wonderful," she said in her quiet voice.

"And during the show we serve a delicious medieval meal," Hannah went on. "Roasted chicken, vegetable soup, and apple tart."

"Now that sounds wonderful to me," said Benny, grinning. Henry, Jessie, and Violet laughed. They knew their little brother loved to eat.

"I bet you'll like it even more when you hear how they used to eat in medieval times," Hannah said. "No silverware. And that's how we do it here. Everyone eats with their hands."

"Even the soup?" Benny asked, his eyes wide.

"You drink it right out of your bowl," Hannah said.

"Wow!" said Benny. "Grandfather would never let us do that at home."

The Aldens had lived with their grandfather since shortly after their parents died. At first the children had run away, fearing their grandfather would be mean. They lived for a while in the woods, in a boxcar from an old train. But once they learned how kind their grandfather was, they came to live with him. He had moved the boxcar to their backyard so they could play in it.

Just then the sound of a trumpet rang

through the air. Hannah looked at her watch. "They must be starting the dress rehearsal for the show. Would you like to come see it? You can be our test audience."

The Aldens' faces lit up. "Sure!" said Benny.

Hannah led the way. The children sat down beside her in the front row. Since this was only a rehearsal, the rest of the seats were empty.

A mandolin player strolled about singing and plucking lively tunes on his mandolin. A jester wearing a brightly colored checkered leotard worked his way around the ring, juggling and doing cartwheels.

When the strolling performers left the ring, the lights in the seating area dimmed and bold music filled the air. The Aldens sat on the edges of their seats, eager to see what would happen next.

One by one, knights on horseback raced in, their shiny armor glinting in the bright arena lights, their colorful capes rippling. Each knight carried a shield and a banner. Each banner showed the knight's symbol—

a lion, an eagle, a castle, a star, or a rearing stallion.

The horses were draped with colorful banners to match the knights' outfits. Some had brightly colored ribbons braided into their tails.

Most magnificent of all was the Silver Knight, who came in last. His banner and his horse sparkled with silver.

As the knights passed by, they waved to the children, who waved back and cheered. The Silver Knight tossed roses to Jessie and Violet.

"I hope the Silver Knight wins," said Benny.

"Me, too," Violet agreed.

Now the knights filed back out of the ring. The music grew quiet. A man in a long black cape entered, carrying a microphone. A lone spotlight shone down on him as he began to speak. "Welcome to our medieval fair, gentlemen and fair maids. I am the master of ceremonies. Let me introduce our noble king, His Royal Highness King Richard."

Spotlights lit up a royal-looking man with a white beard and white hair who was sitting on a throne. He wore a red velvet cape lined with fur. On his head was a crown studded with jewels. The king stood up to greet the audience. He nodded his head as he looked slowly around the darkened arena. The Aldens could see that a sword with a jeweled handle hung from his belt.

Benny whispered, "Wow, is he a real king?"

"No, he's an actor," said Hannah. "His name is Richard Worthington."

"He makes a great king," said Jessie.

"Oh, yes," Hannah agreed. "Just wait until you meet him. He really believes he is a king."

Then the master of ceremonies spoke again from the center of the ring. "Now I present the king's fair daughter, Princess Annabel." A beautiful young woman stepped into the spotlight. She had shining brown hair that fell gently over her shoulders. She wore a long white gown embroidered with silver threads.

"She's beautiful," Violet whispered.

Princess Annabel placed her hand upon her father's outstretched arm. She gazed slowly about the arena, a proud smile on her face. Then she and her father sat down side by side upon their thrones.

"Today the knights of the kingdom will compete for Princess Annabel's hand in marriage," the master of ceremonies continued. "Let the games begin!"

"Doesn't she get to choose who she wants to marry?" asked Jessie.

"I guess not," said Henry.

"I'm glad that's not how women find husbands now!" Jessie exclaimed.

Once again there was the sound of trumpets. The knights rode back into the ring. They competed in several different contests including throwing a pointed javelin at a target and using their long wooden lances to pierce metal rings or hit targets. The knights rode quickly and confidently, and the Aldens were amazed at their skill.

"This is really exciting," Jessie whispered.

During the javelin throw, the Green Knight missed the target completely. "I'm sorry, but we must remove the Green Knight from our competition," the master of ceremonies announced. The Green Knight bowed to the king and princess, who nodded their heads at him. Then he rode around the ring waving. The Aldens cheered as he went by.

The contests continued, and one by one the knights were removed—the Purple Knight, the Red Knight, and finally, the Yellow Knight.

In the end, only the Blue Knight and the Silver Knight were left. As the music grew quiet, the two knights retreated on horseback to opposite ends of the ring.

"Now we begin our final and most dangerous competition," the master of ceremonies announced. "It is now time for the joust."

The two knights on horseback turned to face each other. Each held his lance outstretched in front of him as the two raced straight toward each other.

The Aldens held their breath as the knights came closer and closer.

When they met in the center of the ring, there was a loud crash as the Silver Knight's pole hit the Blue Knight's shield. The Blue Knight lost his balance and fell to the ground.

"The Silver Knight won!" Benny cried excitedly.

But the contest was not over. As his own horse ran off, the Blue Knight reached up and pulled the Silver Knight from *his* horse. The two knights both grabbed for their swords and began to duel.

"Oh, my goodness!" cried Violet. "I'm afraid someone will get hurt."

"Don't worry," Hannah whispered. "The fights aren't real. The swords aren't sharp. The knights figured out all the moves in advance—like a dance. They know exactly what they're doing so no one will get hurt."

But the duel looked so real the children couldn't help gasping or cheering at every move the knights made.

The Blue Knight was a fierce fighter, but the Silver Knight managed to avoid his blade again and again. At last the Blue Knight pushed the Silver Knight down to the ground and stood over him. Now it looked as if the Blue Knight had won.

But suddenly the Silver Knight rolled to the side and jumped to his feet.

The two men began fighting again, when suddenly the Silver Knight's sword snapped. The two knights stood stunned, looking at the broken piece of sword lying in the dirt beside them. They seemed unsure what to do next.

The Aldens looked at one another, wondering what was going on. Until now, everything in the show had run so smoothly.

"Oh, no," Hannah said in alarm. "That wasn't supposed to happen!"

CHAPTER 2

The Winner

For a moment the two knights stood there uncertainly. But the pause did not last long. The Blue Knight dropped his sword, as if by accident. The Silver Knight dashed over to pick it up. He held the sword out boldly in front of him. The Blue Knight removed his helmet and knelt down, defeated. Then he walked out of the ring.

"We have a winner," announced the master of ceremonies. "It is the Silver Knight!"

"Hooray!" cried the Aldens.

The children cheered as the Silver Knight

circled the ring, waving victoriously to the audience. Then he walked proudly up to the king's throne. There he took off his helmet. He knelt down before the king, his head bent.

King Richard rose and slowly raised his sword. The sword shone brightly in the spotlight. The heavy jeweled handle glittered.

"Wow, look at his sword!" said Henry. "I bet that sword won't break."

King Richard lightly touched the sword to the Silver Knight's shoulders. Then he smiled at Princess Annabel and announced, "Silver Knight, as winner of the tournament, you shall marry my daughter." Princess Annabel stood up, smiling brightly. The Silver Knight now stood and took her hand. The king, Princess Annabel, and the Silver Knight all bowed to the audience and walked out. Then all the lights came back on.

"What a great show," said Jessie.

Hannah smiled broadly. "I'm glad you liked it." But her smile quickly disappeared.

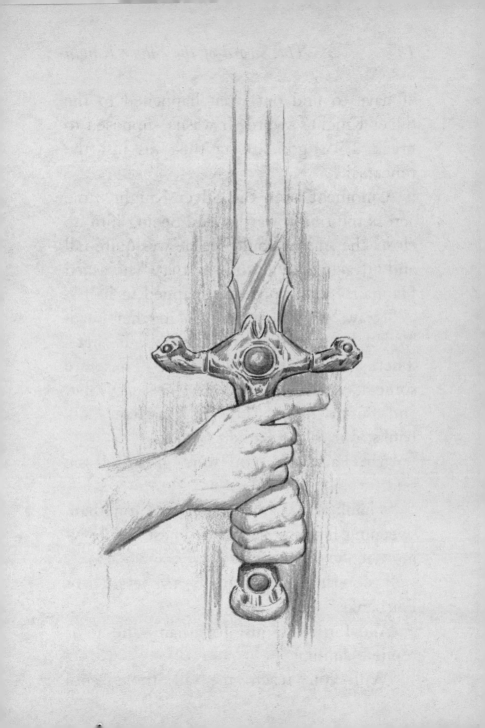

"I have to find out what happened to the Silver Knight's sword. It wasn't supposed to break. It's a good thing this was just the rehearsal."

A moment later, the Silver Knight came across the ring toward them. Seeing him up close, the Aldens could see he was quite tall and attractive "Did you see that?" he asked Hannah. "My sword just snapped in half!"

"I saw," said Hannah, shaking her head. "We'll have to do something about that." Then she turned to the Aldens. "These are some local children, Henry, Jessie, Violet, and Benny Alden. This is Jonathan Fairbanks, our Silver Knight."

"Mr. Fairbanks, you were great!" Jessie said.

"Thank you, Lady Jessie," said Jonathan, sweeping his arm across his chest and bowing deeply.

Jessie grinned. "I'm really just Jessie, Mr. Fairbanks."

"And I'm really just Jonathan," the actor replied, smiling.

"Will you teach me all those cool

moves?" Benny asked, jumping around excitedly, waving his arms as if he were in a sword fight.

"Why certainly, young page, I'd be happy to teach you. But first I need to speak with Hannah." Jonathan turned to her, a worried look on his face. "What are we going to do about my sword tonight? I need a new one."

"We don't have any extras," said Hannah. "That was specially made."

"But how can I fight the final battle without a sword?" asked Jonathan.

"What about the costume shop in town?" Henry sugggested. "They have swords."

"I doubt they'll have one that looks real enough," said Jonathan.

Hannah was silent, trying to think of a solution.

"I have an idea," said Benny. "You could use the king's sword. It was really cool-looking."

A slow smile spread across Jonathan's face. "Yes! That sword would work nicely."

Hannah looked doubtful. "I don't know.

That's a real sword, you know."

"But it's not sharp," said Jonathan. "I won't hurt anyone."

"Still, it's very different from the swords the rest of the knights carry," Hannah said.

"But the Silver Knight is the one who wins the tournament," Jonathan pointed out. "That sword would be perfect. Let's go ask Richard."

"Good luck getting it away from him," Hannah muttered under her breath, but she began walking across the ring to where the actor playing King Richard was standing. He was talking to the actress who played Princess Annabel. Jonathan and the Aldens went with her.

"Richard! Annie!" Hannah called.

The woman who had played Princess Annabel smiled in their direction. The Aldens were surprised to see how tiny she was up close, not much taller than Jessie. Without the lights and grand music, she seemed like a regular woman in a fancy dress. But the man beside her still looked and acted like a king. He turned slowly and bowed his head slightly in Hannah's direction.

"Yes, Madame?" he said in his deep, grand voice.

Hannah smiled and looked at the group around her. "First, let me introduce you to our test audience. This is Henry, Benny, Jessie, and Violet Alden. This is Annie Shore and Richard Worthington."

Annie Shore smiled and said, "Hi."

Richard Worthington held his chin high and gazed down at the children. "You may call me King Richard."

Hannah looked at the Aldens. "See what I mean? He likes to act as if he really were a king."

"My ancestors were knights long ago in England," he explained.

Smiling, Hannah said, "Yes. Well, there's something I'd like to ask you. Since Jonathan's sword broke, can he borrow yours tonight? It's just until we can get him another."

Mr. Worthington's eyes blazed. "Excuse me, Madame, but a king does not give up his sword!"

Hannah sighed. "I knew this would be a

problem," she said. "Richard, I gave you that sword to use when you joined the show. Tonight Jonathan needs to use it."

Mr. Worthington looked angry. "And what will I do at the end of the show, when I bestow my royal honor on him, touching him with the tip of the sword?"

"You can just lay your hands on his shoulders," Hannah suggested. "I think that will be fine."

Mr. Worthington stood and stared angrily at Hannah. Several seconds passed and the children wondered what he would do. At last he unbuckled the belt on which the sword hung. Then he looked sternly at Jonathan. "You'd best be very careful with that sword, young man," he said, his voice low. "If anything happens to it, you will be to blame."

Jonathan nodded seriously, but a trace of a smile was on his face, as if what Mr. Worthington was saying amused him.

Then Mr. Worthington turned to Hannah. "I am still the rightful owner of that sword."

Hannah shook her head. "No, Richard, I

am. Remember, I told you I got it from my parents before they died?"

But Richard Worthington just turned on his heel and strode angrily out of the tent.

As Jessie watched him go, she couldn't help wondering why he was so attached to the sword. It didn't really belong to him.

Hannah handed the sword to Jonathan. She smiled apologetically at the Aldens. "Actors can be very moody sometimes. Especially Richard."

Jonathan studied the sword's handle with the large red gem in the middle. He moved the sword up and down slightly as if measuring its weight. "This is much heavier than the one I was using before," he said. He carefully touched the blade. "Not sharp," he said. He waved it in front of him, a pleased look on his face.

Annie, too, was looking at the sword. "It *is* a remarkable sword," she said. "Where did it come from?"

"My parents collected antiques," Hannah explained. "I found all sorts of things in their attic after they died."

"It looks very valuable," Annie said.

Hannah nodded. "I'm sure it is."

Jonathan smiled broadly, raising his eyebrows. "And now, rightful or not, I am the owner of the sword. It's just what I need. Yes, exactly what I need." Pretending he was sword-fighting, he raced out of the tent.

"I'm glad that's solved," said Hannah. "I just hope nothing else goes wrong."

Violet noticed how tired Hannah looked. "We can help," she offered. "We saw the sign asking for volunteers."

Hannah smiled gently and put a hand on Violet's shoulder. "That's very kind of you, but I think you're a little too young."

"We've helped out in lots of places," Henry insisted. "At an old library, a castle, a museum. We're good helpers."

Hannah looked at the Aldens, her hand on her chin. "What could you do here at the fair?"

"I know how to juggle and do gymnastics. Maybe I could be a jester," Jessie said. "Jessie the Jester." She laughed.

"And I play the violin," Violet said. "I could stroll around playing before the show begins."

"That would improve the show," said Hannah, nodding. "Just one jester and the mandolin player won't be enough when we have a full audience here."

Annie, who had been standing quietly beside them, turned to Hannah. "I need someone to help me dress and do my hair for the show."

"I could do that, too," Violet said.

"Now how about the boys?" Hannah said.

"We're all good cooks," said Henry.

"We can always use more help in the kitchen," Hannah said.

Annie had another idea. "Jonathan mentioned he could use some help putting on his armor."

"Yes, Benny can be a page," Hannah said. "I bet Jonathan will teach you some sword-fighting moves, too."

Benny jumped up and down and spun around excitedly.

"And Henry can be a squire, working with the horses in the stable," Hannah said.

"Great!" said Henry.

"Come on," Hannah said. "I'll show you around."

The children learned that the tent they now stood in was the main tent, where the visitors would see the show. Hannah's office was in a curtained-off section of the main tent. Then she took them outside and they strolled over toward three smaller tents. "These are for the actors who play the knights, king, and princess. This is where they get dressed and wait for the show to begin."

Farther away was another, larger tent. As they walked, Hannah pointed in that direction. "That's where we keep the horses."

A smaller tent nearby held the costumes.

"Where do you make the food?" Jessie asked. She always thought about practical things.

Hannah turned toward a small building next to the main tent. "There's a full kitchen in there—they use it for lots of different events here in the park."

"It will be so much fun to work here," said Violet.

"First you'd better check with your parents," Hannah said.

"We'll ask our grandfather," Jessie told her. "We live with him. But I'm sure it will be fine."

"Bring him to the show tonight," Hannah suggested. "If he says it's okay, you can start tomorrow."

The Aldens hurried out of the tent, eager to get home and tell Grandfather about their new jobs.

When they were halfway home, Jessie said, "We were having so much fun, we forgot to eat our picnic lunch!"

"No wonder I'm so hungry," said Benny.

CHAPTER 3

The Sword

When the Aldens got home, their dog, Watch, came running to the door to greet them.

"Hey, boy!" Jessie said, rubbing his ears.

Watch followed them as they ran to the kitchen where the housekeeper, Mrs. McGregor, was cutting up apples for a pie.

Everyone began to speak at once.

"Guess what's at the Pleasant Valley Park!" cried Jessie.

"You'll never believe what we just saw!" said Henry.

"They had jousting and knights—" said Benny.

"And a beautiful princess," added Violet.

"Wait a minute, wait a minute," said Mrs. McGregor, laughing. She sat down at the table and patted the chairs next to her. "Sit down and tell me what happened. One at a time."

So the children told her all about the medieval fair, the Silver Knight, and King Richard and Princess Annabel.

"The manager of the fair offered us jobs," said Jessie. "Do you think Grandfather will let us work there?"

"I'm sure he will," said Mrs. McGregor. "Call him at his office."

A moment later Henry was on the phone with Mr. Alden, telling him all about the fair. When he hung up, he turned to the others. "Grandfather thought it sounded great. He can't wait to see the show tonight!"

That evening the Aldens returned to the park with Grandfather. They arrived early so they would have time to introduce him to Hannah. They found her in her office in the main tent.

"Hannah Greene, this is our grandfather, James Alden," Henry said.

"Nice to meet you," Hannah said, getting up from her desk. "Your grandchildren are lovely."

"Thank you," said Mr. Alden. "They're very excited about helping here."

"I've saved some seats for you in the front row," said Hannah, leading them to their seats.

The Aldens sat down, and Hannah returned to her office. All around them people were finding their seats. Soon waitresses came in, dressed in long dark skirts and white blouses that laced in the front. They brought platters of food that they placed on the tables in front of each row of seats. The food was delicious—thick vegetable soup, crusty rolls, juicy roasted chicken, and flaky apple tarts. It was fun to drink the soup and eat everything else with their fingers.

As the Aldens were finishing their meal,

the lights dimmed and they heard a trumpet flourish. The show was beginning.

This time the show went smoothly. Jonathan fought the Blue Knight and won, his new sword gleaming in the spotlight. At the end of the evening, since he had no sword, King Richard rested his hands gently on Jonathan's shoulders. The audience cheered and the lights came back up in the tent.

"What did you think?" Jessie asked.

"It was wonderful!" Mr. Alden said. "Very exciting."

"Would you like to meet some of the actors?" Violet asked. "They're all so nice."

"Sure," said Grandfather.

The Aldens left the big tent and stepped out into the night. It seemed very dark after the bright lights inside, and there was even some fog swirling around. As they headed toward Annie's tent, they saw a knight walking far ahead of them. He was headed toward the stable, carrying a large bundle.

"Is that Jonathan?" Benny asked.

"Looks like him," said Jessie. "Same armor and silver jersey.

Benny started running into the darkness, following the knight.

"Wait a minute," Henry said. "No sense running around in the fog. He's sure to come back this way."

When they reached Annie's tent, it was empty.

"I guess she already left," Violet said.

"Let's try to find Jonathan," Benny suggested.

The Aldens walked in the direction they'd seen Jonathan going, but there was still no sign of him. When they arrived at the big tent that served as a stable, they stepped inside. The air smelled strongly of horses. Half walls had been put up to divide the tent into individual stalls for the horses. The men who worked in the stable were settling the horses in for the night. They were pitching hay from a large pile into the horses' stalls. The Silver Knight was nowhere to be seen.

"Did the Silver Knight—I mean,

Jonathan—come in here?" Henry asked the men.

The two men shook their heads. "We've been pretty busy taking the armor off the horses," the taller man said. "He might have come in, but we didn't see him."

"Thanks," said Henry.

"That's strange," said Jessie. "He was walking back this way. Where else could he have gone?"

"There are no other tents back this far," Violet pointed out.

"Well, it's getting late. Time to head home," Grandfather said.

As they left the stable they saw a figure ahead of them, walking away.

It was still foggy on the path, but Violet recognized Annie. "Annie!" she called.

Annie turned around. She seemed startled.

"It's us—the Aldens," said Henry.

"Oh—oh. You surprised me," Annie said, coming toward them.

"Annie Shore, this is our grandfather, James Alden," Henry said.

"I am pleased to meet such an elegant

princess," Grandfather said.

Violet didn't think Annie looked very much like a princess now. She was wearing blue jeans and a T-shirt. Her hair hung limp, with bits of hay in it.

Annie laughed. "It's a fun job. It pays the bills. I'm saving up for college."

"That can be very expensive," Grandfather said.

"Yes," said Annie. "I've been saving for a long time."

"Have you seen Jonathan?" Benny asked.

"Not since the show ended," Annie said.

"We saw him walking to the stable, but then he disappeared," said Jessie.

"We wanted to introduce our grandfather to him," Henry explained.

"Try the knights' tent," Annie suggested. "Good night!" She headed off toward her own tent.

When the Aldens arrived at the knights' tent, Jessie called, "Jonathan, are you in there?"

"Sure, come on in," Jonathan called back. The tent was the size of a large room and contained several chairs and tables. Suits of armor hung on stands throughout the tent. Like Annie, Jonathan had changed out of his costume into jeans and a T-shirt.

"We were following you out toward the stable," Benny said. "But we lost you."

"The stable?" Jonathan looked confused. "I was just in here, changing.

"We want you to meet our grandfather," said Henry. "This is James Alden. And this is the Silver Knight, Jonathan Fairbanks."

"I really enjoyed the show," Grandfather said.

"Thanks," said Jonathan. "You've got some excellent grandchildren."

"And you're an excellent horseman," Mr. Alden replied. "Looks like you've been riding all your life."

Jonathan smiled with pride. "Actually, I just learned for this show. I wanted to be part of this medieval fair so I could . . ." His voice trailed off. He looked as if he had suddenly changed his mind about what he was going to say. He cleared his throat. "Well, I'm glad you enjoyed the show. See you tomorrow." Jonathan walked out quickly. The Aldens were left staring after him.

"That was strange," said Henry. "He was so friendly this afternoon. But tonight he didn't seem to want to talk."

"He's probably just tired," said Grandfather.

Benny yawned loudly.

"Looks as if someone else is tired, too," said Mr. Alden. "Let's go home."

The next day, the Aldens arrived at the park in the mid-afternoon, ready to help with the show. After the successful show the night before, they were surprised to find everyone in an uproar.

"Boy, am I glad you're here," Hannah said when she spotted the Aldens. Her face looked gray and worried. "I don't know what I'm going to do."

"What's going on?" Jessie asked.

Hannah shook her head, gazing off into the distance. "How could I have been so stupid?" she muttered to herself.

The Aldens looked at each other, confused.

"What—?" Violet began.

"I should never have let him use it. I should have known something would go wrong," Hannah went on.

"Let who use what?" asked Benny.

"What's gone wrong?" asked Jessie.

Hannah blinked. "Something terrible has happened," she said. "The sword is missing."

CHAPTER 4

Mysteries Are Our Specialty

"The sword is missing?" Jessie repeated.

"Yes," said Hannah. "We've been looking for it all morning. How could I have used such a valuable sword for our show? It was so foolish of me!"

"Don't say that," said Violet gently. "You didn't know this would happen."

"Anyway, what are we going to do for tonight's performance?" Hannah said. "It was bad enough yesterday having no sword for the king. But the Silver Knight certainly needs a sword. How else can he fight and win the princess?"

"Don't worry about tonight's show," said Jessie. "We'll get a sword."

"But where?" Hannah asked. "We don't have much time."

"We've gotten things for Halloween at the costume shop in town," Henry said. "We'll walk over there right now."

"I guess that is our only choice," Hannah admitted.

"Sure," said Jessie.

Hannah sighed gratefully. "I'll give you some money." She dug into the purse she was carrying. She pulled out her wallet and handed Jessie several bills. "There, that ought to be enough. Buy two swords, so King Richard can have one, too."

Jessie took the money and tucked it into her backpack.

"Where could the sword be?" Henry wondered.

"I don't know," Hannah said, shaking her head. "We've looked everywhere. It's a mystery."

Jessie smiled. "You're in luck. Mysteries are our specialty."

"Maybe we should call the police," Violet suggested.

"I'm afraid that will give our show bad publicity," said Hannah. "People may not want to come if they think there are thieves lurking about. I just wish I had the money to hire a private detective."

"Don't worry," Benny told her. "We'll figure it out."

Hannah's face softened for the first time that day. "I bet you will."

"Before we go to the costume shop, do you mind if we look around a little bit to see if we can find the sword?" Jessie asked.

"I hope you can find it," Hannah said. "I'll be in my office."

When Hannah had left, the children looked at each other.

"Can you believe that beautiful sword is missing?" Violet said.

"What could have happened to it?" Henry wondered.

Jessie pulled a notebook and pen out of

her backpack. She quickly flipped to a fresh page. "Let's figure this out. Who had the sword last?"

"Jonathan used it last night in the show," said Henry.

Jessie wrote that down in her notebook.

"We should talk to him first," said Violet.

The Aldens walked to Jonathan's tent. "Hello?" Henry called, poking his head in the flap.

"Henry, come in," Jonathan said.

When the children entered they found Jonathan sitting in a chair with his feet up on a small table. A magazine was spread across his lap, and he was flipping through it. "What can I do for you? Not time to get ready for the show yet, is it?"

"No," Jessie said. "We just wanted to ask you about the sword you used last night—the one that's missing."

Jonathan turned back to his magazine. "Oh, yes. Too bad," he said.

The Aldens looked at each other, surprised. Jonathan didn't seem upset at all that the valuable sword was missing.

"So I guess you were the last one to have the sword," Jessie went on.

Jonathan looked up. "Yes, I used it in the show—it was great to use a real sword."

"What did you do with it after the show?" Henry asked.

"I returned it to Richard's tent," Jonathan said simply.

"And that's the last you saw of it?" Jessie asked.

Jonathan looked at her and smiled. "Is this an official investigation?"

"Oh, we're just . . . we like to solve mysteries. We're helping Hannah find the sword," Jessie explained.

"I see. Detectives." Jonathan studied the children's serious faces. "I used to like to play detective when I was a kid, too. I played all sorts of things—detective, cowboy, knight in shining armor. I loved to be in disguise, to pretend to be someone I wasn't. I guess I'm still doing that."

"Where exactly did you leave the sword?" Henry asked.

"I put it on Richard's dressing table,"

Jonathan said. "What a cluttered mess! I'm not surprised the sword got misplaced."

"Was he there when you left it?" asked Henry.

"No," Jonathan said. "I'm not sure where he was."

"What time was it?" asked Jessie.

Jonathan thought for a moment. "It was right after the show, probably about ten o'clock. I just left the sword on the dressing table and walked out." He shrugged. "Never occurred to me that something might happen to it." He looked back at his magazine.

The Aldens had no more questions, so they left. "See you later," Benny called.

Outside Jonathan's tent, Jessie made a couple of notes in her notebook.

"Richard Worthington's tent next?" Violet asked. The others nodded, and they set off in that direction.

"We didn't learn much from Jonathan," said Henry.

"Except for one thing," Violet said. "He didn't seem very concerned about the sword."

"No," Jessie said thoughtfully. "He certainly didn't."

A moment later the children were at Mr. Worthington's tent. The flap was propped open, and they could see him inside. The Aldens immediately saw that Jonathan was right—the dressing table was a complete mess, as was the rest of the tent. Piles of clothing and armor and bits of hay were strewn about everywhere.

"Mr. Worthington?" said Henry.

"Yes?" he responded, looking up from a pile of clothing he had been sorting through. He did not seem happy to have visitors.

"We just wanted to talk to you about the missing sword," said Jessie. "If you don't mind."

"I knew that young scoundrel should never have borrowed my sword," Mr. Worthington said. "I warned them something bad would happen."

"Jonathan said he left the sword in here after the show," said Jessie.

"I don't care what Mr. Fairbanks says. When I came in last night, there was no sword," said Mr. Worthington.

"What time did you come back to the tent?" asked Henry.

Mr. Worthington frowned. "I don't know. I don't wear a watch."

"Was it right after the show ended?" asked Jessie. "That was ten o'clock."

"No, I stayed for a few minutes to sign autographs," Mr. Worthington said. "I probably got back here around ten-fifteen."

"Did you look all around here for the sword?" asked Jessie, her eyes traveling around the tent.

"Yes, Ms. Greene and I turned this tent upside down looking for the sword," said Mr. Worthington. "I assure you it's not here."

"I wonder where it could be," said Jessie.

"I suggest you ask Mr. Fairbanks." And with that Mr. Worthington strode angrily out of the tent.

The Aldens all looked at each other, stunned.

"We didn't learn much from him, either," said Henry, sighing.

"No, except that he thinks Jonathan is to

blame," said Jessie, writing in her notebook. She glanced at her watch. "We'd better get to the costume shop or there won't be any swords for tonight's show."

The children had been to the costume shop several times to buy things for their Halloween costumes. It was just a short walk from the park. As they walked, they talked about what could have happened to the sword.

"Do you really think someone stole it?" Benny asked.

"I hate to think that," said Henry. "But what else could have happened to it?"

"Who would have stolen it?" asked Violet.

"Jonathan is the most likely suspect," Henry said. "He was the last one who had it. He says he put it in Mr. Worthington's tent, but no one saw it there."

"Remember how happy he was to get the sword?" Violet said. "He kept saying it was just what he needed."

"I'm wondering if maybe Richard Worthington stole the sword," Jessie said. "He was so angry when Hannah asked him to give it to Jonathan."

"He claimed he was the 'rightful owner,'" Henry recalled.

"A pretty strange thing to say since the sword really belongs to Hannah," Jessie said. "And today he kept saying, 'I warned them something bad would happen.'"

"So do you think that he's just pretending he never saw the sword last night, but actually he's hidden it away somewhere?" asked Violet. "And now he's trying to put the blame on Jonathan?"

"He was very angry that Jonathan was using 'his' sword," said Jessie. "Today he called him a scoundrel. Maybe he wants to get Jonathan in trouble."

"Hannah said Mr. Worthington could be very moody," said Violet. "And he sure seems that way."

They had reached downtown Greenfield. The children walked up Main Street to the corner where the costume shop was.

The store was crowded with costumes of all kinds. There were colorful clown costumes, scary witch dresses, elegant princess gowns, even a furry dog suit.

"Hello," said the man behind the counter. "Can I help you?"

"We need some swords for the medieval fair at Pleasant Valley Park," Jessie said.

"I've heard about that fair," the man said. "So you need something a medieval knight would use?"

"Yes," said Jessie.

The man opened a drawer and pulled out several different swords. One was made of cheap plastic and didn't look real enough. Jessie was also worried it might break, like the first one had. Another sword was too small. After considering all of them, the children selected two sturdy swords with fancy handles.

"These will be fine," Jessie said, taking the money out of her backpack to pay for them.

As they walked back to the park, Benny and Jessie each took a sword and dueled. "These are great," Benny said.

"But nothing like the one that was stolen," said Violet. "It was really beautiful."

"That reminds me," said Henry. "Annie was talking about how beautiful the sword was. And how valuable. Do you think . . . ?"

Jessie stopped dueling. "That Annie stole it?" she asked thoughtfully.

"No!" cried Violet. "Not Annie."

"She was wandering around in the dark last night," Henry reminded her. "She could easily have taken it."

"Jonathan was wandering around, too," Violet said.

"And who knows where Mr. Worthington was," said Benny.

Jessie shook her head. "There's definitely something strange going on at the fair."

CHAPTER 5

Sir Benny

The Aldens brought the new swords to Hannah as soon as they got back to the park.

"These are great," Hannah said as Jessie handed her the money that was left. "You've saved the show."

"Any more news about the real sword?" asked Henry.

"No," said Hannah grimly. She checked her watch. "The show starts soon. I'd better get you all started."

Hannah had found them all costumes to

wear so they would look as if they were from the Middle Ages.

"Boys your age would be training to be knights," Hannah said to Benny and Henry, handing them light cotton pants with tunics over them. "In the Middle Ages, you would really have worn tights, not pants, under your tunics."

Both boys made faces.

"Tights! Those are for girls!" Benny cried.

"I had a feeling you might be more comfortable in pants," Hannah said.

"Thank you." Henry told her.

"Whew!" said Benny.

Hannah gave Jessie and Violet long dresses to wear. The girls changed into their dresses excitedly. They took turns braiding each others' hair, and in no time they looked just like ladies-in-waiting for a princess.

"Another night you can be a musician and a jester," Hannah said, holding up some colorful checkered tights and tunics. "But for now you look just right."

Hannah sent Henry off toward the stable

to help dress the horses in the elaborate gear they wore for the show. Violet and Jessie went to Annie's tent to help her dress. Benny walked off toward the knights' tent to help Jonathan. He was carrying one of the swords they'd bought.

When he entered the tent, Benny was surprised to find Jonathan whistling happily. Everyone else at the fairgrounds seemed to be feeling bad because of the stolen sword.

"Hello!" Jonathan said brightly when he saw Benny.

"I brought you this sword to replace the one that was stolen," Benny said.

"Thanks," Jonathan said, taking the sword. He looked at it briefly. "Nothing like the other one, but it will do for the show."

"Can you believe the other sword was stolen?" Benny asked.

"It's terrible, isn't it?" said Jonathan. But he still didn't really seem bothered. "Let's get going, my young page." He pointed to a pile of clothing and armor he needed to put on before the show.

"What is a 'page' anyway?" Benny asked.

Jonathan was changing from his regular clothes into gray padded long underwear. As he dressed he told Benny all about the Middle Ages. "You know what a knight is, right? Someone who protected the king and the noblemen. If you wanted to be a knight, first you became a page in a wealthy lord's manor. Boys about your age would start off as pages, living with a noble family."

"At my age?" Benny asked. He couldn't imagine being sent away from his own family when he was still so young. He thought for a moment. "What would I do as a page?"

"You'd serve meals and help the lord get dressed each morning," Jonathan said.

Benny made a face. "That doesn't sound like much fun."

"You'd also learn how to ride on a wooden horse and fight with a wooden sword," Jonathan went on.

"Now that's better," Benny said, grinning.

"Then, when you got to be about Henry's age, you'd become a squire," said

Jonathan. "Squires were like assistants—they followed their masters into battle and looked after the horses and armor."

"Henry would like that," Benny said.

"And once you were about twenty-one, you'd be made a knight," said Jonathan.

"How do they make you a knight?" Benny wanted to know.

"There's a special dubbing ceremony," Jonathan said. "Kneel down. I'll show you."

Benny knelt in front of Jonathan.

"Now bow your head."

Benny did as Jonathan told him.

"Now the lord would lightly tap your shoulder with a sword." Jonathan picked up the new sword Benny had brought him and touched it to Benny's shoulders.

"Rise, Sir Benny. You are now a knight!" Jonathan and Benny both laughed. Then Jonathan looked at his watch. "I'd better hurry up—the show starts in half an hour."

"It won't take you that long to get dressed," said Benny.

"Not with your help," Jonathan agreed. "But you know it used to take knights as long as an hour to put on all their armor."

"You sure know all about knights," said Benny.

"I did a lot of reading on the subject," Jonathan said.

"Just for this show?" Benny asked.

"No, actually it was because—" Jonathan began. Then he stopped himself. "We've been talking too much. Come on, help me get ready, or I'll be late."

Benny wondered what Jonathan had started to say. But there was no time to ask. There was too much to do to get Jonathan ready for the show.

First Benny helped Jonathan strap on his leg armor over his long underwear. Next came the breastplate and backplate.

"This is heavy," Benny said.

"And this isn't even real armor," said Jonathan. "Back in the Middle Ages a suit of armor could weigh as much as forty or fifty pounds! I'm glad my costume doesn't weigh that much. It's actually pretty flexible. Even back in the old days it was.

It had to be so that the knights could move around in battle."

"Why did they wear the armor, anyway?" Benny asked.

"To protect themselves from their enemy's weapons," Jonathan explained as Benny helped him put on the pieces covering his shoulders and arms.

Next, Benny helped Jonathan strap on his silvery cape, which fluttered behind him as he walked. Jonathan smiled in the mirror as he combed his hair. "Noble knights of the Round Table, here I come," he said to himself. Last, Benny helped Jonathan put on his long metal gloves and helmet.

"Hand me my sword," Jonathan said just before leaving the tent.

Benny handed him the new sword.

"See you after the show!" Jonathan called out cheerfully.

Benny couldn't believe Jonathan was in such a good mood. Wasn't he at all worried about the stolen sword? After all he'd been the last one seen with it. But for some reason, Jonathan seemed to be happier than ever. Benny couldn't help wondering why.

That night, again the show went well. The two swords the children had bought worked fine, although they lacked the sparkle of the missing sword.

When the show ended, the children changed out of their costumes and left them in Hannah's office. Grandfather came to pick up the children since it was dark out. They piled wearily into the car.

Jessie told their grandfather about the missing sword.

"How terrible," Mr. Alden said. "Hannah must be very upset about the sword."

"Yes, she is," said Violet.

"We promised to help her," Jessie recalled. "Tomorrow we'll have to get to the park a little bit earlier so we can look around. Maybe we can find the sword, or at least get an idea of who might have taken it."

"Good plan," Henry said. "We'll go over there first thing."

CHAPTER 6

In the Kitchen

When the Aldens arrived at the park the next morning, they looked for Hannah. They finally found her in the kitchen building. She was talking to the chef, who was a large man in a white apron and hat.

"I sure am happy to see you!" she called when she saw the Aldens. She motioned for the children to join her. "I think you mentioned that you like to cook?" she asked.

"We love to cook," Benny said. When the children had lived in the boxcar, they had cooked all their own meals, and they still enjoyed cooking together.

"Great," said Hannah. "This is Anthony, our chef."

"And you must be the Aldens. I've heard so much about you," Anthony said.

"I need you to help out in the kitchen. Anthony's assistants didn't come in today," said Hannah.

Anthony explained, "One took the day off for a family emergency, and the other called in sick." He sighed. "How am I supposed to get all the food ready without my staff?"

"Don't worry, Anthony. The Aldens know how to get things done," said Hannah, as she walked out of the kitchen.

Anthony nodded, but he looked as if he didn't quite believe her.

"We need to wash our hands," said Jessie. She was ready to get to work.

"The sink's over there." Anthony pointed. The children washed their hands with soap and warm water. Then they tied on the white cloth aprons Anthony gave them.

"First we need to get the soup ready," said Anthony. "To be really tasty, it needs to simmer for several hours."

Anthony gave Benny and Violet vegetable scrapers and showed them where the bags of potatoes and carrots were. Benny and Violet washed and scraped the vegetables. They handed them to Jessie and Henry, who chopped them on a heavy wooden cutting board. Soon a huge pile of chopped carrots and potatoes filled the cutting board. Benny and Violet threw the long curls of brown potato skin and orange carrot peelings into the garbage.

When Anthony saw how quickly they'd chopped the vegetables, his face broke into a grin. "Great work!" he said. "Hannah was right —you do know how to get things done."

Anthony showed them a large pot of broth on the stove. The children gathered up the chopped vegetables and put them into the pot.

"There, now that can simmer while we prepare the rest," said Anthony. "Of course, if this were a real medieval kitchen, this pot would be hanging over an open fire in a huge hearth. But here, we use a modern stove."

Benny sniffed the air. "That soup smells delicious."

"It was delicious when we had it the other night," said Violet.

Next Anthony got out flour, yeast, salt, and several large bowls. He gave each of the children a measuring cup to fill with water at the sink. Then, following Anthony's lead, the children mixed the dough for the bread. Then Anthony sprinkled flour all over the wooden table, and each of the children took the dough they'd made and kneaded it with their hands.

This was Benny's favorite part. "This feels like molding clay," he said.

After they had kneaded the dough for several minutes, Anthony took the mounds of dough and placed them in large bowls to rise.

"Later, I'll shape the dough into loaves and bake the bread," he explained. "Now all we have left to prepare is the chicken." He went to the large refrigerator and pulled out several trays of raw chicken and some bowls of a reddish-brown sauce. He handed the children large basting brushes. "We're going to brush the sauce onto the chicken before we roast it."

The children dipped their brushes into the bowls and then painted the sauce onto the chicken.

"This is fun!" said Violet.

When all the chicken had been coated with the tangy sauce, Jessie and Henry helped Anthony put the trays back in the refrigerator.

Anthony put his hands on his hips and looked around the kitchen with satisfaction. "We're in good shape," he said. "Nothing else needs to be done right now. Thank you so much for your help."

"It was our pleasure," said Jessie as they left to find Hannah and see what else she needed them to do.

The Aldens found Hannah in her office. "Are you done cooking?" she asked.

"Yes, Anthony said everything was ready," Jessie said.

"Great, because now I need you to find Richard's crown," said Hannah.

"His crown?" Violet repeated.

"You don't think it was stolen, do you?" asked Henry, his voice concerned.

"No, it's just a prop—not valuable at all. Richard is always losing things. He lost his cape earlier this week, and he's had to use a replacement," Hannah said. "He's a bit of a slob."

"We were in his tent last night," said Jessie, nodding.

"So you know what I'm talking about," Hannah said. "He's in the main tent right now, having a cup of tea. I'm sure he won't mind if you look in his tent."

Mr. Worthington's tent was still a complete mess, with piles of clothing everywhere.

"He really is a slob," said Benny. "This room is even messier than mine!"

The others laughed, thinking of Benny's messy bedroom.

"At least you don't have hay all over," said Henry, plucking a piece of hay off a chair.

"Hannah said he is always losing things—

you don't think he could have lost that sword and blamed it on Jonathan, do you?" Violet wondered.

"It's possible," Henry said.

The children set to work looking through the piles.

"Here's the crown," Henry said, picking it up from under a table where it had been left.

"Look at this," said Violet, picking up a heavy book that had been buried underneath a chair. "It's called *The Knights of Old England*, volume 1."

"Cool!" said Henry.

"Can I see?" Benny asked.

The children gathered around Violet, who flipped slowly through the book. It was illustrated with colorful drawings of knights in armor. Violet noticed one marked with a small yellow sticker.

"Look, Mr. Worthington marked this page," she told the others.

"I wonder why," asked Jessie.

Violet scanned the page to see if there was anything unusual written there.

Suddenly she gasped.

"What is it?" Henry asked.

"Maybe Richard was telling the truth," she said. She sounded stunned.

"What do you mean?" asked Jessie.

Violet pointed to a picture of a knight carrying a black-and-white banner with an eagle on it. Then she read the caption below. "Historians believe this flag and emblem were carried by the Worthington family of northern England." Violet looked up from the page. "Maybe one of Richard's ancestors really was a knight."

CHAPTER 7

Investigating

"I thought he just liked to think that his ancestors were knights," said Jessie. "But I guess it really could be true."

Violet slowly turned the pages. There were several paintings of members of the Worthington family. "This is Lady Worthington." Violet pointed to a woman in an elegant dress. "She lived from 1625 to 1693. And next to her is her husband, Lord Worthington."

Benny leaned over to look closer. "Hey,

he does look like Richard Worthington!"

"I don't know about that," Henry said.

"Well, they both have beards," Benny pointed out.

"Is that their dog?" asked Jessie.

"Yes," Violet said, with a smile. "It says that noble families often had portraits painted of their dogs. This one is a springer spaniel named Jeffrey."

"I think we should have a portrait painted of Watch," said Benny.

"I don't think he'd sit still long enough," Jessie said.

"What's that other yellow sticker for?" Henry asked, pointing to a sticker on a page further along in the book.

Violet flipped ahead. The sticker marked the last line of the last page of the chapter. Violet read it aloud to the others, "For more information about the Worthington family, see volume 2."

"What does that mean?" Benny asked.

"Sometimes if a book is really long it's printed in two parts, or volumes," Jessie explained. "Remember this book says volume 1 on it? There's a second book that goes with it."

"Wait a minute. Richard wrote something on this sticker," Violet said, bending her head to look at it more closely. "His handwriting is very messy. I can't read it."

"Let me see," Henry said, taking the book from her. "I have experience with messy handwriting."

"Yes, your own," Jessie teased him.

Henry looked at the tag. "Starts with an *S*." He frowned, puzzling over what the letters might say. Then suddenly he looked up. "I think it says 'sword.'"

Henry handed the book back to Violet so she could look at the word again. Jessie and Benny leaned over her.

"I think you're right," Jessie said. "Richard Worthington seems to be very interested in swords."

Just then the tent flap swung open. Standing in the doorway was Richard Worthington.

"What are you young scamps doing in my tent?" he demanded, peering down at them.

"Hannah told us you couldn't find your crown," Henry said nervously. "She asked us to look for it." His hand shook slightly as he handed the crown to Mr. Worthington.

Mr. Worthington took the crown and placed it on his head. Then he looked slowly from one face to the next. The children wondered what he would say. Finally he spoke. "Thank you for finding it. I must have . . . misplaced it." He stepped out of the doorway and held it open, as if waiting for the children to leave.

Jessie took a deep breath before speaking up. "We also found this book, Mr. Worthington. I hope you don't mind that we were looking through it." She held the book out in front of her.

Mr. Worthington took the book. He raised his eyebrows. "I don't mind. Did you see my ancestors mentioned in there?"

"We did," said Henry.

"Pretty cool," Benny said.

The corners of Mr. Worthington's mouth turned up slightly. "Yes," he said. "Cool. Now I ask that you leave."

One by one the Aldens filed out of the tent.

When they were far enough from the tent that they felt certain Richard Worthington couldn't hear them, Jessie turned to the others. "I would love to know what it says about the Worthingtons in volume 2."

"Me, too," said Henry.

"Looks like we'll be doing some investigating at the library tomorrow," Violet predicted.

That night, Jessie and Violet performed in the show as a jester and a musician. The girls excitedly changed into their special checkered costumes and pointy shoes. They wore hats with long jingling tails. Jessie entertained the audience with lively jumps, cartwheels, and back handsprings. She also juggled apples without dropping a single one. Meanwhile Violet serenaded the audience with her beautiful violin music.

While the girls were busy in the tent, Benny helped Jonathan dress. Henry worked in the stable, preparing the horses.

Once again the children had fun, and the show was a great success. But still there was no sign of the missing sword.

The next morning Mrs. McGregor made the children a hearty breakfast of eggs, bacon, homemade biscuits, and orange juice. As Violet drizzled honey on a biscuit, her eye was caught by a photograph in the morning newspaper, which Grandfather had left on the table. The photo showed a group of knights in armor.

"Hey, look," she said. "There's a picture here of the medieval fair." Then Violet looked closer. "No, wait a minute," she said, reading the caption. "This article is about a medieval movie they're making. It's called *The Noble Knights of the Round Table*."

"Cool!" said Henry. "We'll have to go see that."

"Yes," said Violet, her eyes scanning the article quickly. "It says they're choosing the cast right now, and they are hoping to find some new young actors."

"Hey, I hate to interrupt," said Jessie,

"but remember we are going to the library today?"

"That's right," Violet said, popping her last bit of biscuit into her mouth. "Let's clear the dishes and get going."

At last they were ready to go. They got on their bicycles to ride to the library. They arrived just as the librarian was unlocking the door. "You must really want to get some books!" she said with a laugh.

"One in particular," Jessie said as they followed the librarian back to the main desk. "It's called *The Knights of Old England*, volume 2."

"All right," the librarian said, looking on her computer to find the book. She wrote the location on a small slip of paper and handed it to Jessie. "Go upstairs and you'll find the book there."

The Aldens went directly to the section of shelves written on the paper.

"Wow, look at all these books about knights," said Benny. He pulled out several and sat down on the floor to look at them. They were books written for adults, so he couldn't read them on his own. But they were filled with beautiful illustrations.

Henry spotted *The Knights of Old England*, volume 2, on the bottom shelf. He pulled the book out and carried it to a nearby table. The children all sat down with him.

"Check the index," Jessie suggested.

Henry went to the back of the book and looked in the *W* section for "Worthington." "Here it is," he said after a moment. "Pages 72 through 75 and page 100."

Henry found page 72 and began reading. "This is all about the Worthington estate in northern England," he said. He pointed to a picture of a castle. "This is where they lived in the seventeenth century."

"So that might be Richard Worthington's family home," said Jessie. "Very nice."

"For our family home, they could have a picture of a boxcar," said Violet with a laugh.

Henry read on. "There's some interesting stuff in here, but I don't see anything about swords."

"Try the other entry," Violet suggested. "Page 100."

Henry flipped ahead several pages. On page 95 a new chapter began entitled, "Weaponry." The pages that followed contained illustrations of all kinds of weapons used by knights. There were crossbows and longbows, axes and maces, daggers and shields. Page 100 turned out to be filled with illustrations of swords.

"If we're looking for swords, I think we found them," said Henry.

Each sword was different—some had plain handles, others were elaborately carved. Henry's eyes were drawn to a sword at the bottom of the page.

"Look!" Henry said in amazement. "It's the sword! The one that's missing!"

"Really?" asked Benny.

"Look for yourselves." Henry held the book out for the others to see.

The children leaned over the page, studying the sword.

"It certainly does look like the sword," Jessie said.

"I remember it had that big red stone in the middle of the handle," Violet said, pointing to the picture.

"Yes, I remember that, too," Jessie agreed, handing the book back to Henry.

Henry looked at the page again. "There's something written underneath. It says this sword was given to the Worthington family by the king of England as a reward for bravery in battle. It was passed down from generation to generation. Then about thirty years ago, it was sold at an auction and disappeared from public view. No one knows what happened to it. But it would be worth a lot of money if it were found today."

"Do you remember what Richard said to Hannah?" Jessie asked. "He said the sword was rightfully his. I thought he was just saying that because he wanted to use that sword. But it looks like he might be telling the truth!"

The others were silent, but just for a moment before Benny blurted out, "I bet he took it!"

"He certainly does seem like the most

likely suspect," Henry agreed.

"Jonathan said he gave the sword back to Richard," Jessie recalled. "And no one has seen it since."

"But we don't have any real proof that Richard stole it," Violet said.

"And we also don't know where it is," said Henry.

"We haven't solved the mystery yet," said Jessie.

"But we will," said Benny.

CHAPTER 8

Benny Delivers a Message

That evening, the Aldens went to the park as usual. Hannah greeted them as they came to change into their costumes. "Do you realize we have only two more nights here in Greenfield?" she asked.

"Really?" said Henry. The week had gone by so quickly

"Tomorrow night is our last show here. Then we're moving on to Silver City," Hannah said.

The children dressed quickly and headed off to their various jobs. But before they separated, Jessie turned to the others. "We've got to solve this mystery before the fair leaves Greenfield. We've got to find that sword!"

The others nodded solemnly.

Benny went to his usual job of helping Jonathan prepare for the show. Jonathan was cheerful as always, whistling and joking with Benny. He seemed to love looking at himself in the mirror, especially when he was all dressed up in his armor.

"My, uh, friend is coming to see the show tonight," he told Benny.

"That's neat," said Benny. "I'm sure he'll like it."

"Yes, I think he will," Jonathan said.

When Jonathan was finished dressing, he poked his head out of the tent. Crowds of people were lining up to enter the main tent.

Jonathan called, "Hey, Benny, come here for a minute."

Benny joined Jonathan in the doorway.

"Do you see that man with the beard and the dark sunglasses? He's my—" Jonathan hesitated. "My friend."

Benny noticed that Jonathan had started to call the man by a different word but had stopped himself. He wondered why. Benny studied the crowd. "Yes, I see him."

"I want you to do me a favor," Jonathan said. "Will you give him a message from me?"

"Sure," Benny said, always eager to be useful.

Jonathan leaned his head close to Benny's and spoke in a low voice. "Tell him 'Our plan is working. We're going to be rich!'"

Benny's eyes opened wide when he heard the message.

"Got it?" Jonathan asked.

Benny nodded and swallowed hard. "Okay," he said. "I'll tell him."

As Benny hurried out of the tent, his mind was racing. What did Jonathan mean? Was he talking about stealing the sword? Was this man Jonathan's partner in crime? Benny hated to think of Jonathan that way, but he couldn't help wondering.

Even though he was worried, Benny did as Jonathan had asked. He ran over to the bearded man. "Excuse me, sir," Benny said.

"Yes?" the man replied. He looked surprised.

"I have a message for you from Jonathan Fairbanks," Benny said.

Now the bearded man nodded. "Ah, yes, Jonathan."

"He told me to tell you, 'Our plan is working. We're going to be rich,'" Benny said.

The bearded man smiled broadly. "I'm glad to hear it. And I'm looking forward to seeing the show."

"It's a great show," Benny said. "Goodbye." He went back to Jonathan's tent. What were Jonathan and that man up to, he wondered.

Meanwhile, Violet and Jessie had gone to help in Annie's tent. When they arrived they found her sitting in a chair, gazing blankly into the distance.

"Annie?" said Violet. "Are you okay?"

Annie seemed startled. "Oh, um, hello." She smiled at the girls. "I was just, um, thinking about something . . ."

Jessie noticed a crumpled piece of paper and an envelope in Annie's hand.

"Did you just get some bad news?" Jessie asked gently.

Annie sighed. "Oh, it's just a letter from the bank. I got it a few days ago. I've been trying to get a loan so I can finish college. The bank said no."

"I'm sorry," Violet said.

Annie smiled briefly. "Oh, well, I'll just have to figure out something else."

"Sorry to bother you," Jessie said. "But it's time to get ready for the show."

"I didn't realize it was that late," Annie said, glancing at the small clock next to her mirror. "Yes, I guess you're right."

"Shall we do your hair first?" Violet asked.

"That sounds good," said Annie.

Violet got the brush and began brushing Annie's long brown hair. When she was finished brushing, Violet made a tiny braid on each side, carefully weaving tiny white ribbons into the braids. Then she fastened the braids at the back of Annie's head with a sparkly barrette.

Meanwhile Jessie had been getting Annie's clothes. When Annie's hair was done, Jessie helped Annie into her petticoat and long white dress. It was made of soft velvet, with sleeves that puffed slightly at the shoulders and then narrowed to points over her wrists.

"This is such a beautiful dress," Jessie said. "I love the beading and the silver threads."

"It is a wonderful dress, isn't it?" Annie said. "And certainly more comfortable than wearing armor! I feel so sorry for the men."

"I agree," said Violet. "Armor does not look comfortable at all." She picked up a rhinestone necklace and fastened it around Annie's neck.

Annie laughed. "Trust me, I know. It isn't comfortable. And it's hard to walk in."

"How do you know?" Jessie asked. "Have you ever worn it?"

Annie's face suddenly went pale. "Me?" she asked. "Worn armor? Why would I have worn armor? I just mean, I can tell by looking at it."

Jessie and Violet looked at one another. Why did Annie suddenly seem so embarrassed, as if she'd said something wrong?

"Oh," Jessie said. "That's what I thought."

"I'd better be getting over to the main tent," Annie said, stepping into her white silk slippers. She hurried out, leaving Jessie and Violet behind.

When the children arrived home that night, Grandfather was out at a business dinner.

The children sat down in the kitchen, talking about how much fun they'd been having at the show.

"Don't stay up too late," Mrs. McGregor said, going to her room.

"We won't," called the children.

"This medieval fair has been so great," said Violet. "I wish tomorrow weren't the last day."

"Me, too," said Henry. "Especially since we haven't found that sword yet."

"I know we can solve this mystery," said Jessie. "We've never failed before."

"I could think better if I had a snack," Benny said.

"I had a feeling you might say that," Jessie said, smiling at her brother. "How about some ice cream?"

Benny's face lit up. Jessie went to the freezer and got out a container of mint-chocolate-chip ice cream, while Henry and Violet got the bowls, spoons, and napkins. Benny got the ice-cream scooper.

Soon they were all settled at the table with bowls of ice cream in front of them. Benny stirred his ice cream around and around until it was soft and melted. Violet thoughtfully licked her spoon.

Benny told the others about Jonathan's message that night for the bearded man. "What do you think he was talking about?" Benny asked.

Jessie looked concerned. "I don't know, but it sounds as if he's working with that man, and they stole the sword together. It sounds as if they plan to sell it and get rich."

"Jonathan was the last one seen with the sword," said Henry. "We have only his word that he left it in Mr. Worthington's tent."

"And we saw him wandering around that night," Violet recalled. "Who knows where he was going, or what he was up to. Maybe he took the sword and hid it."

"I don't think it was Jonathan!" Benny said. "I think he's telling the truth—that he left the sword in Mr. Worthington's tent. I think Mr. Worthington hid it somewhere to get Jonathan in trouble."

"That's possible, too," Henry said, eating another spoonful of ice cream.

Jessie pulled out her notebook and looked at the notes they'd made over the past few days. "There's another possibility. They could both be telling the truth. Jonathan said he left the sword at about ten o'clock, right after the show ended. Mr. Worthington was still out signing autographs and thinks he came back to the tent at around ten-fifteen. In those fifteen minutes, someone *else* could have come in and stolen the sword."

"But who?" Violet asked.

"What about Hannah?" asked Benny.

"Why would she steal her own sword?" Henry asked.

"Yeah, that doesn't make any sense," Benny agreed. Violet handed him a napkin to wipe off the ice cream that had dripped on his chin.

"What about Annie?" suggested Jessie. "She keeps talking about needing money for college. She might have stolen the sword for the money."

"She seemed to be covering up something today," Violet recalled. "We started talking about the costumes, and then she suddenly got up and left."

"What do you think she's covering up?" Jessie asked.

Violet shook her head. "I don't know."

"I just have a feeling the sword is hidden somewhere at the park," Henry said. "Maybe the thief didn't have time to take it somewhere else that night."

"Whoever stole it might have buried it,"

Benny said. "That's what you do with treasure."

Jessie and Violet nodded. But Henry looked unconvinced. "I don't know," he said. "If they buried it underground, we'd see a spot that looked freshly dug up. I haven't noticed any spot like that."

"We haven't been everywhere around the park," Benny pointed out.

"We'll just have to search the whole place tomorrow," Jessie said. "It's our last chance."

"That park is huge," said Benny. "How will we ever find it?"

"It's like looking for a needle in a haystack," Violet said.

The Aldens sat quietly for a moment, thinking. Then Jessie stood up and carried her bowl to the sink. "We'd better get some sleep. We'll work on this tomorrow."

The children went off to bed. But Henry couldn't fall asleep. Something about what Violet had said kept going through his mind. "A needle in a haystack . . ."

he mumbled as he drifted off to bed.

In the morning, Henry sat up in bed. He had an idea.

CHAPTER 9

A Needle in a Haystack

Henry ran downstairs to the kitchen, where the others were getting breakfast. "You figured it out!" he told Violet.

"I've figured what out?" Violet asked. She looked at Henry, confused.

"You've figured out where the sword is!" Henry said. "At least, where it very well might be."

"Henry, sit down and explain what you're talking about," Jessie said to her older brother.

Henry sat down, leaning eagerly across the table. "Violet mentioned a haystack. That made me think of the little bits of hay we keep seeing—"

"You mean, like in King Richard's tent?" Benny asked.

"I saw some in Annie's hair one day," Violet recalled.

"Well, maybe that hay is a clue!" Henry said. "A haystack would be the perfect place to bury a sword, wouldn't it? You wouldn't need a shovel, so you wouldn't have to dig."

"Yes, so . . . ?" Jessie asked.

"You saw the haystack inside the stable, which they use to feed the horses. Well, there's an even bigger haystack behind the stable," Henry said.

"So you're thinking the sword might be hidden inside the haystack?" asked Jessie.

"Yes," Henry said. "If Annie or Mr. Worthington put the sword there, some hay might have gotten on their clothes or hair."

"That would explain the bits of hay we've seen," Violet agreed.

The others thought for a moment.

"And it makes sense if Jonathan took it," said Violet. "Remember we saw him heading in the direction of the stable the night the sword disappeared."

"That's right!" said Henry.

"All right, as soon as we get there we'll check the haystack," Jessie said.

When they arrived at the park, they found it was quiet and empty. Most people had not even arrived for work yet. The children headed straight for the stable tent. They could hear the horses whinnying inside.

Just as Henry had told them, behind the tent was a large pile of hay. "Here's the haystack," Henry said. "Let's start looking."

It was a big job. Jessie and Henry pulled handfuls of hay off the pile, making another pile of hay alongside it. Benny and Violet joined in. Benny dropped handfuls of hay on the ground in his eagerness to find the sword.

"Benny, watch what you're doing," Jessie reminded him. "We don't want to make a mess here."

"Sorry," Benny said, trying to be more careful.

The Aldens had moved a large pile of hay when suddenly, peeking out of the hay, they saw a piece of red velvet.

"What's that?" asked Violet.

"I don't know, but it definitely doesn't belong in this haystack," said Jessie.

The children worked more quickly now, shoving hay out of the way until they uncovered a bundle, wrapped in red velvet. The velvet was edged in thick fur.

"Wait a minute," said Violet. "I think that's King Richard's cape."

"You're right," said Jessie. "Hannah mentioned he'd lost it." She picked up the cape and immediately broke into a smile. "There's something wrapped up in here," she said. She placed the bundle down on the pile of hay and began gently unfolding the velvet. "It feels like . . ."

A moment later she had pulled off the last fold of the cape. There, lying in the bundle, was the sword. It looked just as the children remembered it. The large red stone glistened in the center.

"The sword!" Jessie said triumphantly.

"Wow, it really was hidden in the haystack!" said Benny.

"Wrapped in King Richard's cape," said Violet. "Does that mean he's to blame?"

"Maybe," said Henry. "But remember when we saw the Silver Knight that night, he was carrying a bundle. This might be what it was."

"Let's get this back to Hannah right away," said Jessie, wrapping the cape around the sword again. "She'll be glad to see it."

The Aldens went quickly to Hannah's office in the main tent. But there was no sign of her.

"I guess it is still pretty early," Henry said, looking at his watch. "Probably no one will be here for another hour or so."

While the children were waiting, they saw a man parking his car in the parking lot. He was wearing a black jacket and sunglasses. A moment later he was walking toward the main tent, a newspaper tucked under his arm. Suddenly Benny recognized him. "That's Jonathan's friend," he said.

"Can I help you?" Henry called out.

"I'm looking for Jonathan Fairbanks," the man said.

"You can check his tent, but I don't think he's here yet," Henry said. "No one is."

"I just couldn't wait to give him the news," the man said. "Can you give him a message for me?"

"Hey, this is a switch," Benny said, laughing. "Last time I gave you a message from him."

"That's right," said the man. "I knew you looked familiar. I'm Jonathan's agent, Steven Chase. Tell him the movie contract is signed."

"Okay," Benny said. He wondered what the man was talking about.

"Oh, and give him this." He handed the newspaper that had been tucked under his arm to Benny and headed back to his car.

"His agent?" Henry said as Steven Chase walked away. "Why does he need an agent?"

"And what do you think he was talking about—the movie contract?" asked Violet.

Benny unfolded the newspaper Mr. Chase

had handed him. "Local Actor Chosen for Starring Role in *Noble Knights of the Round Table*," the headline read.

Jessie looked at the article over Benny's shoulder. "It's about that movie they're making," she said. As she began to read it to herself, her eyes widened. "Now I see . . ." she said to herself.

"What is it?" Benny asked.

"Just a second," Jessie said, taking the newspaper and flipping the pages. "It's continued on page 10." She opened to page 10 and turned it around so the others could see. There, in the center of the page, was a picture of Jonathan. The caption underneath said, "Jonathan Fairbanks will star in movie."

CHAPTER 10

Noble Knights of the Round Table

"I don't get it," said Benny. "Why is Jonathan's picture in the paper?"

"He got the leading role in that movie, *Noble Knights of the Round Table*," said Violet.

"So that's why he has an agent," said Jessie. "That must be the movie contract Steven Chase was talking about."

"Now we know what Jonathan meant when he said his plan was working and he was going to be rich," said Henry. "He wasn't talking about stealing the sword at all. He was talking about getting the part in the movie and becoming a star!"

"I knew he hadn't stolen the sword!" Benny cried.

"I bet that's why Jonathan was working here—to get practice playing a knight so they'd hire him for the movie," said Jessie.

"He knew everything about knights," said Benny. "I asked him if he'd learned it all to work here and he said no, that he'd learned it for something else. Now I know what!" Benny thought for a moment. "He mentioned this movie, too. He said, 'Here I come, *Noble Knights of the Round Table.*' But I didn't know what he was talking about."

Just then another car pulled into the lot. "Look, there's Hannah!" cried Jessie. Leaving the newspaper on Hannah's desk, she picked up the sword, still wrapped in the cape, and ran toward Hannah's car. The others followed.

"You're here bright and early," Hannah said, getting out of her car.

"We found it! We found it!" cried Benny.

"Found what?" Hannah asked. Then

slowly, a look of hope spread across her face. "You found the sword?"

"Yes, look!" Jessie handed her the bundle.

Hannah placed the bundle down on the hood of her car and began to unwrap the cape. When she saw the sword, her eyes filled with tears. "You found it. You really did."

Hannah hugged each of the Aldens. "Where was it?" she asked.

"It was in the haystack," said Henry. "Out behind the stable."

Hannah frowned. "Whatever was it doing there?"

The children shrugged.

"Someone must have taken it and hidden it there," said Henry. "We don't know yet who or why."

"Well I'm just glad to get it back," Hannah said happily as they walked toward her office. When they'd reached the office, Hannah went to the safe beside her desk. "I'm going to put this sword in the safe right away." When she had shut and locked the door she turned around and looked down at her desk, where the morning newspaper lay. "What's this?" Her eyes widened when she saw the picture of Jonathan. "He's going to Hollywood?"

"His agent stopped by earlier and left that," Henry explained.

"That's great news," Hannah said. Then she sighed. "Great news for him. But I'll have to find someone new to wear the armor of the Silver Knight!" Hannah headed for the door. "I'm going to see if Jonathan's arrived yet so I can congratulate him."

When Hannah left, Jessie turned to the others. "We found the sword, but we still don't know who stole it."

"I don't get it," said Benny. "I know it wasn't Jonathan, but we did see him that night with this bundle."

"No," said Violet slowly. "We saw the Silver Knight."

"That's what I said—" said Benny.

"No," Violet said again. "What Hannah just said made me realize there's a difference. She said she'll have to find 'someone to wear his armor.' That night, we saw someone in the armor of the Silver Knight—but that doesn't mean it was Jonathan."

"You're right," said Henry.

"It could have been Richard Worthington or Annie or anyone!" Benny said. "How will we ever know who it was?"

The Aldens were silent for a moment, stumped.

"Let's go back to the haystack," said Jessie. "Maybe there's a clue there we missed."

The Aldens walked quickly back behind the stable to the haystack. They looked all around, but nothing seemed out of the ordinary.

"I wish I knew what we were looking for," said Benny.

"So do I," Jessie said.

Just then, Henry spotted something shining in the haystack, near the spot where they'd uncovered the sword. "Wait a minute . . ." he muttered, hurrying over. He pushed some hay out of the way and then stood back. "Look at this."

There, partially buried in the haystack was

a suit of armor—just like the Silver Knight's. Jessie helped Henry pull the armor out.

"After they used this disguise, whoever stole the sword hid the armor here, too," Henry said.

Jessie was holding the armor upright beside her. "But look how small it is," she said. "It's barely as tall as me!"

"Who would fit in this armor?" said Henry.

Suddenly Violet realized there was only one person it could be. "It must have been Annie."

"You're right," said Jessie. "She's the only one small enough."

"I can't believe it," Violet said sadly. "How could she do something so terrible?"

"It's a valuable sword, and she said she needed money for college," Jessie recalled. "And the bank refused to give her a loan. That doesn't excuse what she did, but at least it explains it."

"And the sword is still here," Henry pointed out. "She hasn't sold it or anything. So maybe she realized what she did was wrong and changed her mind."

The children walked slowly back toward Hannah's office, carrying the armor. Jessie held the head, Henry the feet.

When they reached Hannah's office, they found a crowd gathered there. Annie, Jonathan, Hannah, and Mr. Worthington all stood around Hannah's desk. Everyone was admiring the picture of Jonathan in the newspaper.

"Did you hear the wonderful news?" Jonathan asked, proudly waving the paper.

But before they could answer, the Aldens saw the smile fade from Annie's face. She grew pale. "You found it," she said. They knew at once that they were right about Annie having stolen the sword.

"Oh, yes, I nearly forgot with all the excitement," said Hannah, spotting the children. "The Aldens found the sword."

"That's wonderful news," said Richard Worthington. "I'm so relieved."

"And we found something else," said Henry as he and Jessie carefully put the armor down. "This was buried in the haystack with the sword."

Hannah looked confused. "That armor?" She came closer to look. "This is one of our smaller suits of armor. I don't understand."

"I can explain," Annie said quietly. "I've been having trouble paying my bills for college. I was desperate for some way to make money quickly. When I heard you talking about how valuable the sword was . . ." Her voice trailed off.

"You stole it?" Hannah asked, her voice full of disbelief.

Annie nodded. "I saw Jonathan leave the sword in Richard's tent that night. No one was around—Richard was still signing autographs. I didn't want anyone to see me, so I ran to the costume tent and put on a suit of armor." She stopped and took a deep breath. "Then I took the sword, bundled it in one of Richard's capes, and hid it in the haystack. I didn't want anyone to see me in the armor, so I hid that there, too."

"We did see a person going toward the stable that night, but we thought it was the Silver Knight," said Benny.

"But why hide the sword?" asked Henry.

"I had just grabbed the sword without thinking what I would do with it. I figured I'd hide it and come back for it later," Annie explained. "Then I knew almost immediately I shouldn't have taken the sword. It wasn't right. But I was afraid to tell anyone what I'd done. I didn't know what to do. I have been trying to figure out a way to return the sword without anyone seeing me."

Everyone was silent. At last Mr. Worthington seemed to step into his role as king. "What you've done was very wrong, young lady."

"I know," Annie said, beginning to cry. "I'm sorry, so sorry."

"Stealing a valuable sword like this, one that has been handed down from generation to generation . . ." Mr. Worthington shook his head.

"I don't know what I was thinking," said Annie. "I'll guess you'll be calling the police now."

"Thanks to these good children, the sword

was returned safely," Mr. Worthington said. He then looked at Annie. "And it seems as though you've learned your lesson." He paused, turning to Hannah. "No permanent harm has been done, wouldn't you agree, Madame Greene?"

"You're right. No permanent harm has been done," Hannah agreed. "The sword is safe. I don't see any reason to call the police. I know you, Annie. You could never have gone through with selling the sword. You would have returned it to me if the Aldens hadn't. I am willing to forget the whole incident."

"Thank you," said Annie, wiping a tear. "I promise I'll never do anything like that again."

"What are you going to do with the sword?" Jessie asked. "We looked it up in a book, *The Knights of Old England*. You know the book, Mr. Worthington. The book said a sword like this one belonged to the Worthington family."

"That is what I have long believed," said Mr. Worthington. "My family may be descended from those same Worthingtons."

"I've been thinking a lot about this sword, ever since it disappeared," said Hannah. "When I found it in my parents' attic, I never realized it was so valuable. I've decided the proper place for it is in a museum, where lots of people can come and look at it. I've contacted a local museum that handles historic objects. I think I will donate it to them."

"That sounds like an excellent idea," said Mr. Worthington.

Annie nodded tearfully.

"How did you think to look in the haystack?" Hannah asked.

"Violet said that finding the sword was like looking for a needle in a haystack," said Jessie.

"And when I started thinking about hay, I realized that big haystack would be a good place to hide something," said Henry.

"How clever of you kids," said Jonathan, who had been quietly listening to everything that was going on.

Everyone seemed to remember that they

had originally been gathered to celebrate Jonathan's movie role.

"Congratulations on getting the lead role in that movie," said Henry.

"You're going to be great!" Jessie said.

Jonathan bowed deeply, as a knight should do. "Thank you, young lads and ladies. It's like a dream come true."

Hannah smiled and shook her head. "I am very happy for you, but I'll miss you. And now I've got to find someone to replace you. Where will I find another knight to take your place?"

While they were talking, Benny had been studying the small suit of armor on the chair. Now he picked up the helmet and put it on his head.

"I know where you can find another knight!" he called out. "Right here!"